SPORTS GREAT

SAMMY SOSA

BASEBALL

SPORTS GREAT JIM ABBOTT
0-89490-395-0/ Savage

SPORTS GREAT BOBBY BONILLA
0-89490-417-5/ Knapp

SPORTS GREAT KEN GRIFFEY, JR.
0-7660-1266-2/ Savage

SPORTS GREAT OREL HERSHISER
0-89490-389-6/ Knapp

SPORTS GREAT BO JACKSON
0-89490-281-4/ Knapp

SPORTS GREAT DEREK JETER
0-7660-1470-3/ Knapp

SPORTS GREAT GREG MADDUX
0-89490-873-1/ Thornley

SPORTS GREAT KIRBY PUCKETT
0-89490-392-6/ Aaseng

SPORTS GREAT CAL RIPKEN, JR.
0-89490-387-X/ Macnow

SPORTS GREAT ALEX RODRIGUEZ
0-7660-1845-8/ Macnow

SPORTS GREAT NOLAN RYAN
0-89490-394-2/ Lace

SPORTS GREAT DARRYL STRAWBERRY
0-89490-291-1/ Torres & Sullivan

SPORTS GREAT FRANK THOMAS
0-7660-1269-7/ Deane

For Other *Sports Great Titles* call:
(800) 398-2504

SAMMY SOSA

WITHDRAWN

John Albert Torres

—SPORTS GREAT BOOKS—

E **Enslow Publishers, Inc.**
40 Industrial Road   PO Box 38
Box 398   Aldershot
Berkeley Heights, NJ 07922   Hants GU12 6BP
USA   UK
http://www.enslow.com

Library of Congress Cataloging-in-Publication Data

Torres, John Albert.
    Sports great Sammy Sosa / John Albert Torres.
        p. cm.—(Sports great books)
    Includes index.
    Summary: A biography of the Chicago Cubs home-run hitter
from the Dominican Republic.
    ISBN 0-7660-2065-7
    1. Sosa, Sammy, 1968—Juvenile literature. 2. Baseball players—
Dominican Republic—Biography—Juvenile literature. [1. Sosa, Sammy, 1968-
2. Baseball players.] I. Title. II. Series.
    GV865.S59 T67 2003
    796.357'092—dc21

                                                    2002006790

Printed in the United States of America

10 9 8 7 6 5 4 3 2 1

Contents

Chapter 1

Home Runs and Tears

Sammy Sosa was already an established superstar home run hitter. After belting 25 or more home runs for the previous five seasons, the Latin-American slugger had little to prove.

Still, despite all the home runs, it was surprising to some during the 1998 baseball season that Sosa was actually challenging perennial home run king Mark McGwire for the league lead. Sosa was a good power hitter, but no one seriously expected him to ever challenge for a home run crown, let alone the all-time single-season record. But by the time August rolled around, it was obvious that the two National League sluggers were set to wage a serious assault on the single-season home run record set by Roger Maris in 1961.

By early September it was clear the record would fall. The only question was who would do it first? McGwire or Sosa?

Sosa had electrified Chicago fans all season by hitting mammoth home runs. Soon, his trademark smile, big swing, and hop out of the batter's box became a nightly sports highlight. Fans would tune in to see who would be the first to break the record. Would it be the mighty McGwire, who played first base for the St. Louis Cardinals? Or would it be the unlikely home run hitter with the big smile, Sosa?

As the season progressed, Sammy began the ritual of blowing kisses toward the sky and pounding his chest after reaching home plate. He said the kisses were directed toward his mother in the Dominican Republic.

On September 8, 1998, Sosa led the Cubs into St. Louis to face McGwire's Cardinals. Sosa had 58 home runs while McGuire had 61. McGwire quickly ended some of the drama when he became the first of the two to belt home run number 62, breaking the record. The redheaded home run hitter hugged Sosa after hitting the historic blast. The two men, from very different cultures and backgrounds, had become close friends during their quest for the record. Both players expressed the highest regard for one another all season long.

But after the celebrations, there was still a home run crown to claim. Just a few days later, Sammy Sosa went on a home-run hot streak. Like most power hitters, Sosa's home runs seem to come in bunches. In fact, in the month of June alone, Sosa made headlines everywhere by smashing 20 home runs. For some ballplayers, it takes a full season to hit as many as 20 home runs.

Sosa had already belted three homers in the three-game series against St. Louis to tie the old home run record. He was not done. No one could tell how badly Sammy Sosa wanted to hit home run number 62 by looking at his face. As usual, the Dominican outfielder strode to the plate against Milwaukee's Eric Plunk with a huge smile and a swagger that fans had responded to all season. He looked as if he were feeling no pressure at all. The crowd, on the other hand, was bursting with emotion. There was an electricity in the air as fans clamored and begged for Sosa to hit one out. He did not disappoint.

Sosa dug in against the right-handed Plunk and unleashed that tremendous home run swing. The ball seemed to explode off of his bat. There was no doubt about

Sammy Sosa had proven himself as a solid power hitter prior to the 1998 season. Still, most fans were surprised to see him challenge the all-time single-season home run record that year.

home run number 62—a 434-foot shot that tied McGwire for the league lead.

The crowd of 40,846 went wild. They gave Sosa a six-minute standing ovation and three curtain calls before the game was allowed to continue.

Sammy Sosa waved to the crowd and blew kisses up toward the fans. That's when the tears started. Sosa tried his best but just could not contain his emotion. Tears of joy came streaming down his smiling face.

"I've never been so emotional," he said after the ballgame. "When I got 62 I have to say it was unbelievable. It was something that I couldn't believe what I was doing."

A few minutes later the tears started yet again when Sosa received a congratulatory phone call from Randy Maris, son of the late Roger Maris, the former record holder who had hit 61 round-trippers for the New York Yankees in 1961.

McGwire finished the season with 70 home runs and Sammy closed out with 66. Baseball fans will remember that incredible display of power for decades to come.

"It's a beautiful year," Sosa said. "Whatever [else] happens in 1998, this is going to be the year that nobody is going to forget what Mark and I have done."

During the final days of Sosa's home run barrage on history, Hurricane Georges devastated his native country of the Dominican Republic. Sosa had even taken a call from Dominican President Leonel Fernandez, who assured Sosa that the tiny Caribbean island would somehow make it through the storm. The president told Sosa to concentrate on hitting home runs and to play his game.

But Sosa spent his spare time telephoning family and friends in his homeland to make sure they were okay. Feeling helpless as he learned of death, despair, and chaos, Sosa decided to do something to try and help from the United States.

Prior to the 1998 season, the single-season home run record was held by Roger Maris, who had hit 61 home runs in 1961. Sosa hit his sixty-second home run of the 1998 season in mid-September against the Milwaukee Brewers.

"I have to do everything I can to help my people," he said. "I have to try and find the strength to play a good game tonight."

That was the night he belted his sixty-sixth home run, a 462-foot blast to left-center field against Houston pitcher and fellow countryman Jose Lima. For a moment, Sosa led the league in homers. But forty-five minutes after the Cubs' game finished, McGwire hit his sixty-sixth. Then McGwire went on a home run tear to finish the last weekend of the season. He hit two home runs on Saturday and two more on Sunday, the final day of the season, to finish with an even 70 for the year.

History had been rewritten by two different men during the same season. However, Sosa's home run race with McGwire told only part of the story that was the 1998 baseball season.

Almost single handedly, Sosa had put the Cubs—long a laughingstock in the National League—in their first playoff race in years. But it went further than that. Sosa's boyish enthusiasm, charitable work, and charm had earned him millions of fans as he became one of the most popular players in all of baseball.

Some observed that Sosa might have won the home run crown ahead of McGwire if the Cubs had not been involved in a playoff race. With the Cardinals eliminated from play-off contention by September, it seemed as if the pressure was off McGwire to help his club win. All he had to worry about was hitting home runs. Sosa, on the other hand, was a different story. He would hit behind the runner or try to take pitches to right field for base hits in order to help his team win games. Unlike McGwire, Sosa could not swing for the fences every time he came up to bat. In fact, all season long he told reporters that he was much more interested in the playoff race than in the home run race. Meanwhile, McGwire's manager, Tony LaRussa, admitted during the

Sosa does his trademark hop out of the batter's box after launching a home run.

final week of the season that McGwire's home run chase had become the most important thing to his ballclub.

"Sosa the player was magnificent," wrote *Sporting News* writer Michael Knisley. "Sosa the man was better. He was everything baseball needed in its summer of joy." In fact, some players even publicly wished that Sosa's great attitude would rub off on other big leaguers.

"He [Sosa] has a little boyish enthusiasm that maybe a lot more guys should have," said former teammate Brian McRae, perhaps referring to McGwire, who seemed to be under a lot of pressure to break the record.

Sosa summed it up best himself. "I'm having fun," he said. "This is the best year of my life and I'm enjoying it. I come to the ballpark every day like a baby . . . I'm having so much fun."

Perhaps a hard look at Sosa's past can help explain why this smiling, hulking outfielder has so much fun playing a game for a living. During the heart of 1998's home run chase, Sosa was asked if he was starting to feel the pressure. He smiled that big smile everyone was already used to.

"Pressure?" he asked. "People talk to me about pressure. Pressure for me was when I didn't have food on the table and I had to go through the streets as a shoeshine boy or washing cars, trying to make money for my mother."

The former skinny, malnourished child from the small town in a small country had certainly come a long way from shining shoes.

"When I was back home a long time ago," he said, "when I was a shoeshine boy, I was not thinking of being in the major leagues. But now I'm in the major leagues, and anything can happen."

Anything indeed. Sammy Sosa was now a baseball legend.

Chapter 2

Growing Up

Samuel Peralta Sosa, or Sammy, as he was later known, was born on November 12, 1968, in the tiny village of Consulo in the Dominican Republic. Consulo sits on the outskirts of San Pedro De Macoris, a bigger city that suffers from a great deal of poverty. Major league baseball has seen quite a number of very good baseball players come from San Pedro De Macoris.

The Dominican Republic is a country that occupies the eastern two-thirds of the Caribbean island known as Hispaniola. The tiny Republic of Haiti occupies the western part of the island.

Sugar, tobacco, and coffee are the main money crops for the Dominican Republic, where the language spoken is Spanish. However, many of the small farms that dot the island nation have a difficult time sustaining themselves.

Sammy Sosa was the fifth of seven children born to Lucrecia and Juan Inez Montero Sosa. When Sammy was very young the family moved to San Pedro De Macoris. The children grew up in extreme poverty and things only got worse when Sammy's father passed away. Sammy was only seven years old at the time. The children had to grow up largely on their own, because Sammy's mother had to work full time just to keep the family fed.

The family lived in a two-room apartment in a building that had been converted from a hospital. Sometimes,

Sammy and his brothers would take turns sleeping on the floor because there was not enough room for all of them on the bed. And even though the family did not have a television of its own, Sammy loved to watch cartoons when he could. In fact, during the home run chase of 1998 a reporter asked Sammy to name his first love. Sammy's response? Cartoons, of course.

Sammy—whom friends nicknamed Mikey for some strange reason—and his four brothers spent a lot of time shining shoes for pennies and selling orange juice and washing cars to help raise money for their mother.

"We were poor," Sosa said. "We definitely were poor."

One thing that just about all of the children in the Dominican Republic love to do—once their chores are finished, of course—is play baseball. The Dominican Republic is a tropical island, so the temperatures rarely dip below 80 degrees, making it a place where baseball is played all year round. Many on the island view baseball, and sometimes boxing, as the only ways to escape a life of poverty.

As a child, Sammy dreamed of being a boxer, but his skinny frame did not promise to turn him into a powerful fighter. That, plus the fact that his mother once told him she could never bear to watch him fight, helped him focus his attention on baseball. The major problem with playing baseball, however, was that equipment was very hard to come by because the majority of parents could not afford to buy gloves, bats, and balls for their children.

But like so many kids in Latin American countries, the will to play baseball is stronger than the harsh realities of poverty. Sammy and his friends found ways to fashion baseball equipment from a variety of different everyday items. Sammy used to fashion baseball gloves from milk cartons and carve tree branches to make his own baseball bat. If milk cartons were scarce, a regular cardboard box would do the trick for those needing a baseball glove.

Sammy Sosa was born in the small village of Consulo in the Dominican Republic.

The ball was the easiest thing to make. The boys would take a rolled up sock and continue to put tape around it until it became the same size and shape as a baseball.

Longtime major-league infielder Tony Fernandez, also from the Dominican Republic, once pointed out a cardboard box to several sports reporters and explained to them that he could make four baseball gloves out of the small box. He explained that they would cut a piece of cardboard and then tie it onto their hands with a piece of string.

So Sammy would run home from school, take care of any responsibilities he had, and then play baseball until the sun went down. In addition to his love of the game, there was another inspiration for Sammy to keep playing baseball. He would see Dominican ballplayers like George Bell and Pedro Guererro come home after the major league season had ended and they would be wearing beautiful clothes and jewelry. They drove big cars and they never had to worry about money.

Sammy would tell his friends that this was the same lifestyle he wanted. He dreamed of playing in the big leagues. He was not afraid to tell anyone who would listen that one day he would return in a big fancy car with loads of jewelry, too. Most of his friends laughed or scoffed at the notion. But that only made Sammy even more determined.

One of Sammy's idols while growing up was his brother, Luis. Sammy would follow Luis around wherever he went and also looked up to him as a great baseball player. Sammy was not the only one who thought so. Word spread throughout the small island of the great baseball player Luis Sosa. Soon major league scouts began following him and Luis even earned himself a tryout with a major league team. But all the scouts were in agreement on one thing: Luis was too small to ever be a successful big league player.

So Sammy's older brother decided to coach Sammy and encourage him to give baseball a real shot. He talked

Sosa's family was very poor growing up. Unable to afford baseball equipment, Sosa would fashion himself a bat and gloves from a variety of everyday items.

Sammy into joining organized leagues when Sammy turned fourteen. Sammy joined several leagues in the nation's capital of Santo Domingo, mainly for fun. But he also held out hope that one day he would become a professional baseball player.

It was in these leagues that Sammy, fourteen, gripped and swung his first real baseball bat. Hitting a real baseball with a real baseball bat and watching it travel to the outfield was a new feeling for Sammy—a feeling that he never wanted to lose.

"I didn't play on a real team until I was fourteen, when my brother talked to me about being ready to play with them," Sosa said years later, after making the big leagues. "I played baseball when I was little, but only in the streets. The streets were dirt. We didn't have gloves, we just used our hands. Instead of a ball we'd take a sock and roll it up. We used sticks for a bat."

Naturally, there were no cleats. Until Sammy joined those organized leagues he had played ball in his bare feet.

Luis took Sammy to the man he would later credit with teaching him to become such a great hitter. The man's name was Hector Peguero. Peguero founded several baseball leagues in the area and even coached eleven teams at once all by himself. He was known around the neighborhood as Baseball University.

Peguero is credited with being the person to convince Sammy to swing hard and swing big every time he was up. It was Peguero's belief that Sammy was such a slow runner that he would never make it to the big leagues as a spray hitter. No, Sammy Sosa would have to be a power hitter.

Sammy and Peguero would spend hours every day refining his game, working at his swing and learning how to play the outfield. Hector Peguero became a sort of surrogate father to Sammy. Peguero was the only one who understood why Sammy needed to talk so big and brag about how he would make the big leagues all the time. He was there when the other kids would tease Sammy for his stuttering or for the way he fumbled over words and did not articulate himself well. It was Peguero who knew how hungry Sammy was every night as he waited for his mother to come home from work with just enough money for the day's only meal. Sammy would sometimes play baseball to forget how hungry he was. In a poor nation, Sammy was on the bottom rung of the poverty level. His family was always a meal or two away from starvation.

Peguero had a large family of his own and had a hard enough time providing for them. So he helped Sammy the best way he knew how: teaching baseball. For Sammy, it was a different type of nourishment. For the next two years, Sammy tore up the baseball leagues with his raw talent.

Nearly 200 of Hector Peguero's players had wound up signing professional contracts with major league organizations, but only three had made it briefly to the major leagues. But Peguero knew Sammy was something special when he saw the fifteen-year-old slam a ball out of Rico Carty Baseball Field and into the window of an apartment across the street. (Rico Carty was a former Dominican major league all-star from the 1960s and 1970s.) Many people, and Peguero in particular, were awed by the display of power this short skinny teenager was able to display.

By the time he was sixteen years old, many people began noticing how "Luis's little brother" was actually a great baseball player in his own right. People recognized that Sammy, or Mikey as they called him, had a real hunger for baseball. His passion for making the major leagues was intense. He had others convinced as well. Luis Sosa worked two jobs so that Sammy would not have to. He wanted his younger brother to concentrate on just playing baseball.

Then came the opportunity of a lifetime.

Like many of his countrymen, Sosa saw a possible career in Major League Baseball as the best way to escape poverty.

The Texas Rangers were one of many major league teams that had begun taking a much more aggressive approach to recruiting Latin American baseball players for their organizations. For many years the Latin American market was virtually untapped by the major leagues. Only the greatest of the Latin ballplayers were ever discovered. Now there seemed to be much more of an effort to find players with potential that would benefit from the coaching, training, and facilities available in the United States. Many teams now had their own Latin American scouts scouring the tiny Caribbean countries for ballplayers.

Omar Minaya was a professional scout for the Rangers who had heard of Sammy Sosa. He invited Sammy to an official tryout, along with some other local kids he deemed worthy. The problem was that Sammy would have to take a five-hour bus ride there and he did not have good baseball equipment for the tryout. He was leery but also knew that he would probably never come as close as this to realizing his dream.

So Sammy woke up early that morning and, nervous as he was, kissed his mother goodbye and went off in pursuit of his big-league dream.

Chapter 3

Minor Leaguer

Sammy Sosa is lucky that the scout who invited him to try out was Omar Minaya. Minaya, who later became general manager of the Montreal Expos, is regarded as one of the brightest baseball minds in the game. He was the first Latino general manager for a major-league team.

Sammy Sosa was lucky that Minaya was able to see beyond his deficiencies and recognize the makings of a great ballplayer.

Because Sammy had lived in poverty for so long, he was severely malnourished. After the long bus ride, an exhausted Sammy also had very little power. He hit very weak ground balls and his throws from left field bounced a few times before reaching their target. Sammy was sure that he had failed the tryout. But Minaya saw something different.

"He was a frail kid with big hands and big feet," Minaya said. "He worked out with some dirty baseball pants, old shoes with holes in them and a real thin baseball shirt with holes in it. But I saw athletic talent and I saw courage. I saw a guy who was not afraid to air it out and to play, I saw bat speed and I saw a good arm."

It was Sammy's hunger and desire that impressed Minaya the most. He was impressed with the kid, who was not embarrassed by his clothes or his situation—a kid who just wanted to play baseball.

He decided to offer Sammy a contract.

But in typical Sammy Sosa fashion, Sammy felt he was worth more than Minaya was offering.

Minaya offered $3,000 but Sammy was holding out for $4,000. After a solid half-hour of negotiations the pair settled at $3,500. Again, Minaya was impressed.

"I liked that about him," Minaya said. "He had a great desire to play professional baseball, but he wasn't just going to go. He had some principles, and he felt he was worth a little more than I was offering him."

Sammy signed on the dotted line on July 30, 1985, and was now part of the Texas Rangers organization. In a few months he would be leaving home for life in the United States. So what does a sixteen-year-old kid who has known nothing but poverty his whole life do with $3,500? Sammy bought himself a used bicycle and then gave the rest of the money to his mother.

Even though Sammy was nervous about going to a foreign country all by himself—especially one that spoke a different language—he never let it show. Sammy was his usual confident self.

"It was tough for me. But when you're a gladiator you don't worry about things like that," he said. "You've got to do what you've got to do. All I need is God, myself, a glove and a bat."

Sammy's mom was afraid for her son but Sammy was happy that he would finally be able to help his family by sending them money from the United States. The Rangers assigned Sammy to a rookie league team in the Gulf Coast League. And while Sammy played well and advanced his game on the field, he was reluctant and afraid to learn to speak English. Although he shared an apartment with a few other Latin ballplayers, Sammy was embarrassed to speak English in front of anyone. In fact, when he and the other ballplayers would go out to dinner, Sammy would let one of

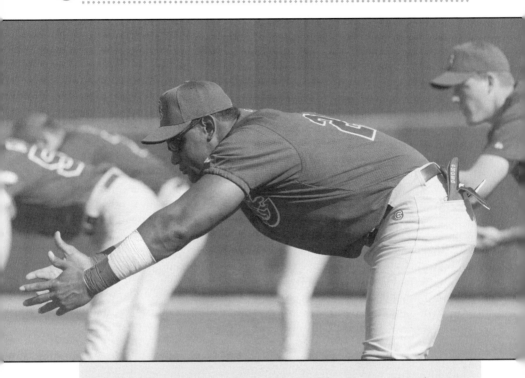

Sammy Sosa signed his first professional contract with the Texas Rangers in July 1985.

the other players order dinner and then would nod his head signaling that he would have the same thing to eat.

Sammy's troubles translated onto the field as well. Because Hector Peguero had taught him to be such a free swinger, Sammy was impatient at the plate. He chased bad pitches and struck out an awful lot. He was also not yet strong enough to hit home runs. In fact, he was struggling just to get hits in rookie-league baseball, the lowest level of the minor leagues.

Sammy had some good company on that rookie-league team, however. Among his teammates were future major-league stars Juan Gonzalez, Wilson Alvarez, and Dean Palmer.

At the end of the season, Sammy returned to his family in the Dominican Republic. At the behest of the Texas Rangers, Sammy played winter baseball for the team in Santo Domingo, his nation's capital. It was there that Sammy kept working hard and started to develop his body.

For Sammy, who never played organized baseball until he was fourteen years old, it was simply a matter of trying to play as much baseball each year as he could. The thinking on the Rangers' part was that the more baseball Sammy could play, the better he would become.

Sosa never lost the confidence of scout Omar Minaya and slowly began to improve as he moved his way up through the Texas Rangers organization. Still, whenever Sosa began struggling he would fall back into his old habit of swinging too hard and chasing bad pitches. Even when he made contact with a badly pitched ball, he would hit it weakly. Luckily for Sosa, Minaya understood the way Latino ballplayers think and play and convinced the Rangers to have patience with the youngster from the Dominican Republic.

"You've got to understand something about Latin players when they're young—or really any ballplayers from low economic backgrounds," Minaya said. "They know the only way to make money (and help support their families) is by putting up offensive numbers."

Sosa did not make a lot of money playing minor league baseball. Still, he would send his mother and family almost everything he earned. He wanted them to rise above the bitter poverty that he grew up in.

By the time the 1989 baseball season started, the Rangers had already promoted Sosa to their AA team in Tulsa, Oklahoma. Sosa was starting to feel more comfortable in the United States and much more comfortable playing baseball for a living.

When his minor-league career began, Sosa had a bad habit of swinging too freely. This made him more prone to strike out.

By June 16, Sosa was tearing the cover off the ball. He was batting .297 when the Rangers decided to call him up to the major leagues. Even though Sosa was nervous, he did not let it affect his play. He slashed two base hits in his very first game against the New York Yankees.

Less than a week later Sosa belted his first major league home run, a shot off of future Hall-of-Famer Roger Clemens, who was then with the Boston Red Sox. But Sosa's play eventually tailed off. After a 25-game cup of coffee in the majors he was sent back down to the minor leagues. (When players spend a short time of the season in the major leagues, it is sometimes referred to as a "cup of coffee.") Sosa batted only .238 during that twenty-five-game stretch, but he was not disappointed. In fact, those twenty-five games with the Rangers proved to be just what he needed. He rededicated himself to working even harder on his hitting and his fielding. Sosa was determined to be the best player that he could possibly be.

Sosa began going to the ballpark earlier than his team-mates to take extra batting practice. He would also ask coaches to hit him fly balls and line drives in the outfield. Sosa would then practice hitting the cut-off man from the deep outfield to strengthen his arm. When there was no one around to help him, Sosa would hit balls off the batting tee all by himself.

His hard work did not go unnoticed. Larry Himes, the general manager of the Chicago White Sox, was scouting some minor leaguers when Sosa caught his eye. Himes liked the way the ball popped off of his bat, but more importantly, he loved Sosa's work ethic. He saw a player who did nothing but hustle every time he was on the field. He saw a hungry young ballplayer who wanted nothing less than to be a success in the major leagues.

So on July 29, Himes traded all-star outfielder Harold Baines and utility man Fred Manrique to the Rangers for

Sosa played in his first major league game for the Rangers in 1989. He stroked two hits against the Yankees in the game.

Sosa, pitcher Wilson Alvarez, and infielder Scott Fletcher. Sosa reported to the White Sox's AAA team in Vancouver, Canada. His work ethic and hitting skills impressed his new manager, Marv Foley, who said Sosa had the skills to be a great one. Foley was not Sosa's manager for long, however. Sosa played so well at Vancouver that less than two weeks after being traded to the White Sox, he was called up to play for the big-league club. In his first game with the White Sox, Sosa had 3 hits, including a home run.

Future U.S. President George W. Bush was the owner of the Texas Rangers when the White Sox acquired Sammy Sosa. Later, he would often joke that the worst decision he ever made was letting his general manager trade away Sosa.

Even though Sosa had a hot start for his career as a member of the White Sox, his development was very slow. He still tried to hit a home run every time he came to bat and his play suffered.

In 33 games with the White Sox, Sosa batted a respectable .273 with 10 RBI, but he was still swinging too hard. Sosa did show some power, with 3 homers and 5 doubles out of his 27 hits. But he would also allow his struggles at the plate to affect his concentration in the outfield. He soon earned the reputation of being a poor fielder, something that he has worked hard to change over the years.

Despite his troubles at the plate and his clumsiness in the outfield, the White Sox saw enough in Sosa to name him their starting right fielder for the 1990 baseball season. Sosa also began to feel comfortable in Chicago as he learned to speak English. He was also earning a big enough paycheck to send a lot of money home to his mother and his brothers and sisters. Sosa was able to take care of his family by playing baseball.

Sosa's dream had come true.

Chapter 4

Major Leaguer

The year 1990 was Sosa's first as a major league starter. Even though the White Sox gave Sosa the full year to assert himself as a big league force, the youngster did struggle some of the time. It was, however, his few glimpses of greatness that convinced the Chisox to keep Sosa in the lineup.

Sosa showed some of his power potential, slamming 15 home runs, but was still inconsistent at the plate, hitting only .233. What was also disturbing to the White Sox was that Sosa walked only 33 times in 579 plate appearances. That meant Sosa was still swinging at too many bad pitches and was not showing enough discipline at the plate. Swinging at a bad pitch or not working a pitcher deep into the count often results in the batter falling behind in the count. This forces the batter to take a defensive approach to hitting as opposed to an offensive approach.

Part of why Sosa was struggling with his batting average so much was because of the approach of his hitting coach, Walt Hriniak. The well-known Coach Hriniak stressed hitting the ball where it was pitched. He wanted his hitters to deliberately try and hit to the opposite field and pick up punch, or "bloop," base hits. For a young, raw hitter like Sosa, it was frustrating to try and cut back on his swing.

Despite all this, it still had to be considered a successful rookie season for the Dominican outfielder. In fact he was the only American League player to reach double figures in doubles (26), triples (10), homers (15), and stolen bases (32).

Chicago General Manager Larry Himes said he knew Sosa would be a good player when he traded for him—he just did not think he would be that good so fast.

In 1991, Sosa had one year under his belt and was assured that he would remain the team's starting right fielder for the season. And after an off-season of playing ball and lifting weights in the Dominican Republic, Sosa felt great and was indeed in terrific shape for the start of the 1991 campaign.

But things deteriorated shortly after the start of the year. Sosa could not get used to the idea of cutting down on his swing. Soon, he was confused every time he came to home plate. He started striking out far too often. By the end of April, Sosa found himself out of a starting job and was riding the bench.

Sosa became depressed. He would rather have been playing every day in the minor leagues than not playing at all in the majors. At least there, he thought, he would be able to play every day and get better. The team kept him in the majors, however.

In May, Sosa made the most of his new part-time status when he won a pair of extra-inning games with home runs. But in June, Sosa slumped very badly. By July, the team had no choice but to send him down to the minor leagues and hope that he could work out his hitting problems.

Sosa played well enough in the minor leagues to get called back in mid-August. Sosa told friends and teammates that he worked very hard in the minors and did not want to go back down. But Sosa did very little to distinguish himself before the season ended. His final numbers were not good: He batted only .203 with 10 home runs and 33 runs batted in.

In 1989, Texas traded Sammy Sosa to the Chicago White Sox. Sosa earned a spot as a starting outfielder for the Chisox in 1990.

After two and a half seasons, the White Sox were ready to give up on Sosa and let someone else fill his right field position. Luckily for Sosa, one of his biggest fans was still Larry Himes, who had now taken a similar job with the cross-town Chicago Cubs.

Himes traded one of Sosa's childhood idols, George Bell, to the White Sox for Sosa and a minor league pitcher. Sosa was excited about the chance to start over with a different team. He was also amazed that he was traded for someone he had once washed cars for.

"Everything happens for a reason," Sosa said. "George, I used to wash his car. Unbelievable! It's an unbelievable world."

With the Cubs, Sosa had the confidence of a general manager that had traded for him twice. His free-swinging style would no longer be restricted by his hitting coach. His new comfort level resulted in a more relaxed Sammy Sosa. This translated into a higher batting average.

Another thing that may have helped Sosa mature was the fact that he got married that off-season to his teenage sweetheart, Sonia Esther. Although Sosa had yet to prove himself as a great player, he was established enough to help his family back home and start one of his own.

That June, Sosa was already off to a fine start for the Cubs when he came to bat against Montreal's ace pitcher Dennis Martinez. A fastball got away from Martinez and Sosa could not get out of the way in time. The ball slammed into Sosa's right wrist, breaking it.

Sosa was forced to spend five weeks nursing the wrist back to health. When he finally came back it seemed as if he did not miss a beat. Sosa blasted a home run on the first pitch he saw after the injury. But then, 10 games later, Sosa fouled a ball off of his left ankle. He tried to stay in the game but X-rays showed a broken bone. Sosa was done for the season.

Sosa makes a leaping catch of a fly ball up against the ivy covered wall at Wrigley Field in Chicago.

Sosa batted .260 with 8 homers and 25 RBIs in only 67 games. More importantly, Sosa had solidified his position with the Cubs. He did not have to worry about a starting job. Sosa would man right field for the Cubs for years to come.

Sosa took advantage of the opportunity. He electrified fans with his swagger, his smile, and, most of all, his power and speed. In 1993, Sosa became the first player in Cubs history to hit more than 30 home runs and steal more than 30 bases in the same season. To celebrate, Sosa bought himself a medallion on a chain that said 30–30.

"People might have wanted so much from me before, and I might have tried to do for them what I wasn't ready to do," Sosa said. "But I work hard every day. I think I'm doing what a lot of people wanted me to do, though."

His manager, Jim Riggleman, agreed with Sosa's assessment.

"Our expectations are so high for him that there is no way he can live up to everyone's expectations on a daily basis." Riggleman said. "But he does put together those long stretches when he does put together some phenomenal things."

Sosa batted a very respectable .261 in 1993 and drove in 93 runs, finally proving himself to be a genuine home run threat. And even though he was out from under the tutelage of Walt Hriniak, Sosa's numbers did become more selective at the plate, and he even started hitting outside pitches to the opposite field.

In 1994, Sosa was on his way to another great year when the Major League Players Association voted to go on strike and cancel the last part of the season. But Sosa was still able to put up great offensive numbers, belting 25 round-trippers, driving home 70 runs, and stealing 22 bases. That was a season that most baseball fans would like to forget because there was not even a World Series.

Sosa and his Cubs teammates congratulate each other after a win.

But fans welcomed back the players in 1995 and Sosa did not disappoint. Despite missing more than 20 games with an injury, Sosa had a great season, belting 36 home runs and driving home 119 runs. Because of his fine performance, Sosa was chosen to his first All-Star team. He also stole 34 bases that year, marking his second 30–30 season.

Sammy Sosa, the poor kid who used to shine shoes, sell oranges, wash cars, and use a cardboard box for a baseball mitt, was now a major league All-Star. He was also very rich.

It was important for Sosa to be accepted as a great player—not only by the people of his own country, but by everyone who loved baseball. So Sosa worked hard to learn English and wanted to set an example for everyone.

"I try to do the best I can as a professional," Sosa said. "I try to be the best player I can be to set an example for everybody. The way you set an example is first by the way you play, the way you do your job on the field. That's the most important thing."

It seemed to work. Soon Sosa became one of the most popular players in Cubs' history. Sosa would arrive early and sign autographs, make public appearances, give to local charities, and simply have fun playing baseball. The fans noticed and showed their appreciation by supporting Sosa's every move.

Expectations ran very high for Sosa for the 1996 season, but not very high for the Cubs. The team, which had not won a World Series since the early part of the twentieth century, was not very good and most people had them picked to finish last. But Sosa did not let the lack of a supporting cast affect his play.

He still worked hard, he still played hard, and he still had fun doing it. It definitely showed in his play. Sosa's body developed further as he worked out lifting weights. His strength greatly increased. The people across the street from Chicago's Wrigley Field can attest to that. Sosa broke

Sammy Sosa chugs around second and digs for third. In 1995, Sosa had his second season of more than 30 home runs and 30 stolen bases and was selected to his first All-Star team.

several windows that year, much to the delight of Cubs' fans, who were amazed at Sosa's power.

Sosa was off to his best season ever when once again he was hit by a pitch and forced to miss the rest of the year. Sosa had already belted a career-high 40 homers by mid-August when a pitch by Florida's Mark Hutton broke a bone in Sosa's right hand. In addition to his 40 home runs, Sosa had already driven in 100 runs as well. He was indeed a superstar. Who knows what sort of numbers Sosa would have been able to put up had he not missed the final 38 games of the season?

Sosa told everyone at the time of the injury that he was more determined than ever to get back on the baseball field and perform.

"I have to take it like a man," said Sosa of the injury that ended his run at a home run title. "This isn't an end to my career. I'll come back."

There was some concern by those in the Cubs' organization that the injury to his hand could signal the end to Sosa's career. After all, he had already broken the same wrist. Some doubted that he would come back and be as good as he had been.

They were right. Sosa would not be as good as he had been. When he came back, he would be even better.

Chapter 5

A New Sammy

Sammy Sosa worked hard to rehabilitate his injury in the off-season. He worked out and kept his weight down. Sosa loves Latin food, which can sometimes be very fattening. Because of that, Sosa sometimes needs to work extra hard to stay in shape.

"In the off-season I lift a lot of weights," Sosa said. "I work out a lot, sometimes I get a little overweight."

Sosa sometimes jokes that his favorite restaurant is simply ordering room service from the hotel whenever the Cubs are on the road.

Sosa came to spring training in 1997 looking and feeling great. The Cubs, who had made some moves in the off-season to strengthen the club, were expected to be serious contenders for the National League Central title—or at least wildcard contenders. The team looked good during spring training in Arizona, and hopes ran high.

Once the season started, however, it seemed as if everything went wrong for the Cubs. The team started out by losing its first 14 games of the season. Sosa batted just .214 over that stretch and showed some of his old habits by swinging at balls out of the strike zone.

Sosa may have been distracted by contract negotiations that were going on. Sosa's contract was running out and he was hoping that the Cubs would sign him up for years to come with a long-term contract. Sosa was pressing as the Cubs and Sosa's representatives worked on a deal. The contract could also give Sosa the financial security he had been looking for.

On June 27, with the Cubs mired in last place, the team signed Sosa to a four-year, $42 million contract. This made Sosa the third highest-paid player in baseball at the time.

Sosa, who had treated himself to a used bicycle when he signed his first professional contract with the Rangers, treated himself to something more extravagant this time around. He bought a sixty-foot yacht and called it "Sammy Jr."

"People always talk about the millions of dollars," a happy Sosa said after signing the deal. "This is not my type of thing. Money doesn't mean anything. I'm here because I play good."

But the money was important to Sosa. He was finally able to ensure that he could take care of his mother and grandmother for the rest of their lives.

Sosa rebounded from the rough start and finished the season with 36 home runs and 119 runs batted. He also reached a personal milestone on August 24 when he slammed his two-hundredth career home run, against Montreal's Steve Kline. It would be the first of many important milestones to come.

With the peace of a long-term contract and financial security, Sosa was ready to concentrate on baseball. He was about to treat the fans to the most amazing four years of home run hitting power of all time. It was a new Sammy Sosa that would explode upon the baseball world.

When Sosa reported to spring training in 1998, he worked closely with hitting coach Jeff Pentland. The two decided to come up with some goals that Sosa should shoot for during the season. They came up with three specific targets: hit for a .300 batting average, score 100 runs, and

In an effort to break his habit of swinging at pitches out of the strike zone, Sammy Sosa set the goal for himself to walk 100 times in the 1998 season.

walk 100 times. That would take a lot of work on Sosa's part since he had always been such a free swinger. Remarkably, there was absolutely no talk of home runs. The hitting coach did this on purpose because whenever Sosa—like most hitters—tried to hit home runs, he usually ended up swinging too hard and striking out.

Pentland and Sosa watched videotapes of hitters like Atlanta's Chipper Jones and then the Cubs' Mark Grace as they batted. Pentland wanted Sosa to see how relaxed they were while batting and hoped that Sosa could pick some of that up. They then devised several hitting drills designed to make Sosa more patient at home plate—something they worked on before each and every game.

The new approach paid off right away. By the end of May, Sosa was hitting well above the .300 mark and already had 13 home runs. In most years that probably would have been enough to lead the league as the baseball season headed into June. But 1998 was anything but a normal season. St. Louis Cardinals first baseman Mark McGwire already had 27 round-trippers as he was about to assault Roger Maris's single-season home run record of 61 homers set in 1961.

But Sosa was not the only reason that Chicago Cubs fans were excited. The team had made some big moves in the off-season. They picked up hard-throwing closer Rod Beck from the San Francisco Giants, slugger Henry Rodriguez from the Expos, and shortstop Jeff Blauser from the Atlanta Braves. Flame-throwing rookie Kerry Wood had also joined the team.

Sosa said the improved team made it easier for him to do his job. He was more relaxed and was able to play better.

"There was too much pressure last year," Sosa said. "I felt if I didn't hit a home run, we wouldn't win. Now I don't feel that anymore."

In June 1998, Sosa set a new record for home runs in a single month by belting 20 round-trippers.

From May 25 to June 21, Sosa put together the most impressive home run hitting barrage in the history of the game. He belted 21 home runs in 22 games. Sosa wound up smashing 20 home runs during the month of June, breaking the record of 18 home runs hit in one month set by Rudy York in 1937. Suddenly, Sosa had thrust himself into the home run race. He and McGwire became the first two players ever to reach 30 home runs before July 1.

As the summer progressed, both McGwire and Sosa belted home runs at a record-setting pace and set the world's baseball fans on fire with their power display. While McGwire and Sosa became good friends during their historic home run chase, the two men acted very differently during their quest. McGwire struggled with the increased attention put on him and admitted to not liking the extra pressure. But Sosa just put on a big smile and let himself enjoy the momentous season.

"It's amazing to me. When I was dreaming, I was dreaming just to make it to the major leagues, not to be the man I am right now," he said.

On August 19, in a game against the Cardinals, Sosa belted his forty-eighth home run of the season to momentarily pass McGwire for the league lead. But McGwire belted two later in the game to claim the lead once more.

Sosa's personality helped him win fans everywhere— even at other teams' ballparks. In one game, on September 16, a packed crowd at San Diego's Qualcomm Stadium gave Sosa a standing ovation when he came to bat with the bases loaded. When Sosa slammed the ball into the second level of the left field grandstand for his third grand slam of the season, the fans went wild. The fans even called Sosa out of the dugout for a curtain call. He happily obliged.

But nowhere was Sosa more popular than at Chicago's Wrigley Field, especially in front of the right field bleachers. Sosa stands at attention and salutes the so-called

Sammy Sosa poses for a photograph with two young fans before a game. Sosa's incredible 1998 season sparked tremendous excitement across the baseball world. Even on the road, opposing fans would offer standing ovations for the slugger.

"bleacher bums" before every game. Sosa loves Chicago and his fans, too. Sosa and his wife live in the Chicago area during the season and raise their four children, Keysha, Kenia, Sammy Jr., and Michael, there. During the off-season the Sosa family travels back to the Dominican Republic. His mother no longer lives in their old two-room apartment. Sosa had a beautiful home built for her.

On September 20, the Cubs celebrated Sosa's incredible season with a "Sammy Sosa Day." The ball field was adorned with flags from the Dominican Republic and celebratory Dominican music blasted from the speakers.

When Sosa hit his sixty-second home run shortly after McGwire belted his record-breaking shot, Baseball Commissioner Bud Selig presented Sosa with the Commissioner's Historic Achievement Award. Members of Roger Maris's family were present at the ceremony in which Selig praised Sosa for his dignity as well as his play.

One week after the standing ovation in San Diego, Sosa belted home runs 64 and 65 against the Milwaukee Brewers, tying legendary slugger Hank Greenberg's 1938 record of 11 games in a season with two or more homers.

Throughout the exciting home run chase, Sosa was even more concerned with trying to get the once-hapless Cubs into the playoffs. He was often called upon to hit the ball to the opposite field or hit behind the runner in order to help the Cubs win. Unlike McGwire, whose team was well out of playoff contention, Sosa could not afford to swing for the fences every time he was up. Sosa repeatedly said during the season that he was much more interested in helping to get the Cubs into the playoffs than winning the season home run title or breaking Maris's record.

McGwire finished the momentous season with 70 while Sosa slammed 66. But the season was not over. Sosa and the Cubs finished tied with the San Francisco Giants for

Sosa points to the sky as he crosses home plate after belting another homer.

the final available playoff spot and were forced to face the Giants in a one-game playoff to advance to the postseason.

Sosa proved that he was no longer just a power hitter but instead an all-around player when he ripped 2 hard singles and scored 2 runs in a 5–3 playoff-clinching victory. Sosa had established himself as a total superstar that season and, more importantly, had helped make the Cubs serious contenders once again.

The Cubs lost in the first round of the playoffs, but Sosa's final numbers were staggering. He finished the season with 66 home runs, 158 runs batted in, 73 walks, and a .308 batting average. He was the landslide winner of the National League's MVP award, receiving 30 of a possible 32 first place votes. Mark McGwire finished a distant second.

Chapter 6

Unfinished Business

Sammy Sosa's breakout season was just the start of a stretch of incredible power and domination the game has rarely seen. In fact, people would begin talking about Sosa in the same breath with baseball legends like Babe Ruth, Hank Aaron, and Roberto Clemente. But that is not all that Sammy Sosa is about. Despite his tremendous athletic abilities and the swagger and the smile, Sosa is much more.

Just ask the people helped in the medical clinic Sosa paid for in the Dominican Republic. The clinic is located at the 30–30 Plaza, named for Sosa's 30-home run 30-stolen base seasons. Sosa also purchased hundreds of computers for the schools in his native land, as well as ambulances and rescue equipment. At the 30–30 Plaza is a statue of Sosa in a fountain known as the "Fountain of the Shoeshine Boys." All the coins donated to the fountain are distributed among the local shoeshine boys. This was Sosa's idea, because he once shined shoes, too. As he had promised, Sosa would never forget his humble beginnings and the people of his homeland.

Sosa also started a charity that benefits American children. In 1997 he began distributing toys to schools and hospitals in underprivileged areas as part of a project he calls "Sammy Claus." Shortly after his historic 1998 season, Sosa also started the Sammy Sosa Foundation. This organization raises money for poor children in Chicago and in the Dominican Republic. Sosa has also worked closely with government agencies in the United States and the Dominican Republic to sponsor immunization programs for children.

The Most Valuable Player award was not the only honor Sosa was given in 1998. He and Mark McGwire were chosen as the 1998 Sports Illustrated Sportsmen of the Year. Additionally, Sosa was awarded the Roberto Clemente Award for his work on and off the field. The Clemente award is given annually to the player who best exemplifies the spirit of Roberto Clemente, a Hall of Fame player who died in a plane crash delivering supplies to earthquake victims in Nicaragua on December 31, 1971. In fact, Sosa wears No. 21 on his jersey in honor of Roberto Clemente, who wore No. 21 while playing for the Pittsburgh Pirates.

But despite the awards, there was still a lot of unfinished business as Sosa continued to strive to make the Cubs a World Series-caliber team. The 1999 season seemed to many a continuation of the spectacular 1998 home run race. This time it was Sosa who got off to a quick start, belting home runs at a near-record pace. On Sept. 18, Sosa became the first player ever to hit 60 home runs in two different seasons when he blasted a round-tripper over the center-field fence in a losing effort against the Milwaukee Brewers. The fans gave Sosa a standing ovation that lasted several minutes.

Despite losing the home run title to McGwire again, 65 to 63, Sosa was proud to be the first to reach 60 once more—a feat that even the great home run hitter Babe Ruth never accomplished. Babe hit 60 in one season and then hit 59 in another.

"I have to say that what I've done today is actually more special than what happened last year," Sosa said after the historic home run. "Mark [McGwire] did everything first last year. He was the man. This year, the record is mine. It's something no one else has ever done. I'm extremely proud of that."

The 2000 season was another first for Slammin' Sammy Sosa. Despite the Cubs having a terrible season and taking a huge step backward from a shot at the title, Sosa once again slammed home runs in bunches. He wound up with 50, an incredible number that somehow seemed small compared to the totals of the two previous seasons. Yet those 50 dingers were enough for Sosa to finally lead the league in home runs.

The Cubs finished last in the National League Central division and were tied with the Philadelphia Phillies for the worst record in the National League, at 65–97. Although Sosa was proud of his accomplishment, he found it hard to celebrate after such a dismal season by his team.

"When the team loses 90-some games, no one can look good," Sosa said. "Even with the year I had, it's not a good year because winning means everything."

Sosa's fiftieth that season, hit on September 16 during a 7–6 loss to the St. Louis Cards, made Sosa the second player to hit 50 or more home runs in three consecutive years. The only other player to accomplish that was Mark McGwire, who battled injuries all season and did not seriously contend for the home run title. It would be the beginning of the end for McGwire, who had to battle chronic back and leg problems as he got older.

The 2001 baseball season was in many ways just as special as the 1998 season—for all of baseball as well as for Sosa. Winning the 2001 All-Star Game home run derby was only a small part of the season for the incredible Sammy Sosa, who was now a fan favorite in every city he

In addition to his many accomplishments on the baseball field, Sammy Sosa has also contributed a great deal of his time and money to charitable causes in both his native Dominican Republic as well as the United States.

visited. Not only was there an incredible three-way home run race between San Francisco Giants outfielder Barry Bonds, Sosa, and the Arizona Diamondbacks' Luis Gonzalez for most of the season, but the Cubs were in the playoff hunt all year. The season would also be the last one for three baseball legends: Cal Ripken, Jr., of the Baltimore Orioles, Tony Gwynn of the San Diego Padres, and McGwire all decided to retire at season's end.

Once again, Sosa finished second in the home run title race—this time to Bonds, who shattered McGwire's record of 70 in a season by belting 73. But there were still plenty of milestones for Sosa. On Sunday, August 26, Sosa hit his fiftieth and fifty-first home runs of the season during a 6–1 Cubs victory. The two shots once again put Sosa in very exclusive company: It made him only the third player ever to hit 50 home runs in four different seasons. The only other two players to accomplish the feat were McGwire and Ruth.

"I'm not going to lie to you," Sosa said after the game, which kept the Cubs in second place behind Houston. "I am very happy to be in that category with Mark McGwire and Babe. But I've still go to continue. I'm not satisfied right now, the season is not over yet and we have a mission to finish in first."

A few weeks later, Sosa became the only player in the history of the game to hit 60 home runs in three different seasons. He wound up hitting .328 with 64 home runs and an astonishing 160 runs batted in for the year. And just like in 1998, Sosa thrived when the pressure and the attention was put on Bonds and not on him. Even though he was involved in a playoff hunt and record-setting home run race, Sosa insisted it was nothing like 1998.

"I'm in a different world right now," he said. "That was exciting and it was something I'll never forget. But this is nothing like that. That year, everybody was getting to know

Sosa dives back to first base ahead of the tag of Cardinals first baseman Tino Martinez during a game in 2002.

who Sammy Sosa is. Now they know who I am. This is different. It's more calm. I'm not worried about the home run thing, or Barry Bonds. I just want to win."

Sosa's Cubs just missed making the playoffs in what was a very tight wildcard race in the National League. Sosa also finished second in the Most Valuable Player voting to Bonds.

Sammy Sosa promises to keep Cubs fans happy for years to come with his special brand of baseball excitement. Just before the 2001 season started, the Cubs rewarded Sosa with a four-year, $72-million contract. This means Sosa will most likely finish his career as a Cub— something that makes both Sosa and his fans very happy.

"I love playing for the Cubs, and love playing at Wrigley Field," Sosa said. "This is my home."

One thing that would not be the same was the legendary Sammy Sosa-Mark McGwire rivalry. McGwire, plagued by injuries and slowed by age, had walked away from the game because he felt he was not able to produce as he had in the past. Sosa said that he would miss competing against his friend.

"He is one of the greatest right-handed power hitters I have ever seen," Sosa said. "I consider Mark a friend. We got close when we shared the home run race in 1998. He must have a good reason for his decision. He's a great person and a great ambassador for the game of baseball. I am going to miss him and baseball will miss him . . . I will never forget him. He will always be in my heart."

A day after McGwire officially retired, Sosa's thirty-third birthday celebration was interrupted by some terrible news. A plane full of Dominicans and Dominican Americans crashed in New York City just after taking off on a flight to the Dominican Republic. Hundreds of people died in the crash that was ultimately ruled an accident.

Sosa shares a laugh outside the batting cage with manager Don Baylor (left) and former Cubs great Ernie Banks (right) in 2001.

"Today is my birthday—now I will associate tragedy with my birthday," Sosa said. "So many Dominicans as well as Americans lost their lives today. My country is devastated."

Barring major injury, Sosa is sure to make the Hall of Fame and compile some of the most impressive numbers in home-run-hitting history. Those he has touched over the years—from the shoeshine boys in San Pedro de Macoris, to the bleacher bums who talk to Sosa before every game, to those he has helped with his numerous charities—know that he is already a hall-of-fame–caliber person. And that's more than enough for Sammy Sosa, the skinny kid who scrounged for change by shining shoes and washing cars and dreamed of making it big.

"What you see now, you're going to see twenty years from now," Sosa said. "The fans understand that I am happy all the time. I've been making a lot of people happy, and I'm happy for that opportunity. I'd like them to remember the way I played the game. Remember me as humble, as a gladiator. Remember me the way I was."

Career Statistics

YEAR	TEAM	G	AB	R	H	2B	3B	HR	RBI	SB	AVG
1989	Texas/ Chicago (AL)	58	183	27	47	8	0	4	13	7	.257
1990	Chicago (AL)	153	532	72	124	26	10	15	70	32	.233
1991	Chicago (AL)	116	316	39	64	10	1	10	33	13	.203
1992	Chicago (NL)	67	262	41	68	7	2	8	25	15	.260
1993	Chicago (NL)	159	598	92	156	25	5	33	93	36	.261
1994	Chicago (NL)	105	426	59	128	17	6	25	70	22	.300
1995	Chicago (NL)	144	564	89	151	17	3	36	119	34	.268
1996	Chicago (NL)	124	498	84	136	21	2	40	100	18	.273
1997	Chicago (NL)	162	642	90	161	31	4	36	119	22	.251
1998	Chicago (NL)	159	643	134	198	20	0	66	158	18	.308
1999	Chicago (NL)	162	625	114	180	24	2	63	141	7	.288
2000	Chicago (NL)	156	604	106	193	38	1	50	138	7	.320
2001	Chicago (NL)	160	577	146	189	34	5	64	160	0	.328
Totals		1,725	6,470	1,093	1,795	278	41	450	1,239	231	.277

G = Games
AB = At-bats
R = Runs
H = Hits

2B = Doubles
3B = Triples
HR = Home runs
RBI = Runs batted in

SB = Stolen Bases
AVG = Batting average

Where to Write Sammy Sosa

Mr. Sammy Sosa
c/o The Chicago Cubs
Wrigley Field
1060 W. Addison Street
Chicago, IL 60613

On the Internet at:

http://www.mlb.com
http://sports.espn.go.com/mlb/players/profile?statsId=4344

Index